The Boss

JINGS CHEN

PARTRIDGE

A Penguin Random House Company

To order additional copies of this book, contact
Toll Free 800 101 2657 (Singapore)
Toll Free 1 800 81 7340 (Malaysia)
orders.singapore@partridgepublishing.com

www.partridgepublishing.com/singapore

For My Dear Late Wife Raquel Susana Czertok With Love Forever

Buenos Aires, South America
Present Time

Dick Williams drove his second hand just rent
Ford 1993 red sports car floating into the car wave along the famous 9 de Julio Avenue, he switched his car radio on a very smooth volume waiting on the intersection of the world widest avenue and Corrientes street, the main street of B.A.'s downtown.

It was 10:30 A.M., The City began turning into it's real rush hours.

Luis Miguel's romantic waterfall voice calmed Dick's nerves. He just got off his midnight flight at 12:30 P.M. The Airport bus sent him to Columbia Hotel one hour later after his arrival to Ezeiza International Airport. Dick recalled his last trip to B.A. was in 1978, almost 26 years ago, the Airport had changed a lot, people here too. This is South America, everything is quieter since this country has just met it's great economic crisis and social difficulties.

As a private detective, he had been almost in the major cities throughout the world and he had also traveled most Latin American countries. Dick received the phone call of his Bureau Chief from Mexico two days ago while he was in his short vacation on Costa Rica's beach side.

"You have to go to B.A. right tomorrow. Dicky." His chief said to him via satellite mobile phone, "Your expenses will be paid in B.A.'s City Bank, the rest things you have to arrange as soon as your arrival, over!" Chief Thompson cut the communication as he usually did.

The traffic sign changed in green at last. Dick stepped on his pad and took advantage to follow close the car riding before him. The aged Ford didn't obeyed his conduction very much.

"Shit! What's a waste-iron. It costs 2 dollars in States." He smiled scornfully to himself.

"Hey, Boludo, que esperas. Dale . . . . , Boludo!" his neighbor behind already threw him a set of Spanish breakfast words.

He looked at the Argentine middle aged driver closed behind him through the front mirror, he just showed his middle-finger outside his left side car window and put his car right into the center driveway heading to Avenida de Mayo about few blocks away.

He easily drove through Avenida de Mayo, then followed a few blocks up to Belgrano Avenue in order to avoid the one-way difficulty. He took out from his Summer jacket pocket the address he just copied through the phone call with Diana Martinez, who was the young executive secretary of Mexico

Embassy in B.A. city, the paper slip was Café Monza's breakfast ticket, where he wrote down the place Diana gave him this early morning: *Avenida de Mayo 658, 7 Piso, Capital Federal.*

He should turn on into Avenida Belgrano then drove down four blocks and cross into left street to reach back Avenida de Mayo where he could find the right number he was going to find out.

"Espero en mi oficina a las 11 horas, esta bien?" Diana made an appointment with him through the call, now it was about 10:50 a.m., he lost ten more minutes on the traffic sign waiting.

Dicky found the right number along the left side of Avenida de Mayo. He parked his car right along the sidewalk and ready to get off.

"Buenos dias, senor." An all assed fat policeman approached his car window and greeted him with his fat palm.

"No se puede estacionar de aca en esta hora." The blue uniformed cop looked at this Yankee's face and discovered that he seemed like a new comer.

"United Nations reporter, sir." Dicky showed his forged U.N.'s I.D. and looked back at the fat cop in a very pride manner.

"Baja de su auto, por favor. Senor. Estamos en la Republica Argentina."

The cop ordered Dick with his fat finger.

Dick got no choice, then he took off his white jacket and obeyed the order.

"Puede ver su pasaporte, por favor. Senor."

"Yes, I'm Americano."

Dick wanted to save his situation with his Yankee's I.D.

"Todo los pasaportes son igueles." The cop showed a pleasant expression.

Dicky found his dark blue passport handed it over to the cop.

The fat cop just copied his name and I.D. No. into the traffic fine form, then tore it up.

"Vd. Tiene 15 dias para pagar la." The cop gave the yellow ticket to Dicky then left.

"Son of bitch." Dicky fucked to the cop in distance.

"Shit." He folded the ticket and got off the car.

Dicky parked the car well and dropped in the café, he headed to the counter and order the bartender a cup of 'café express'.

The fat bartender served him the hot coffee and said, "Un peso y medio, senor.'

He drunk rapidly his hot coffee and threw a two Argentine Peso note on the counter.

"Keep the change." He said and left out.

The building where was the Mexico Embassy was just the building next to the coffee shop. He run into the first elevator he met and buttoned the No.7

The elevator was almost empty except of one middle young lady, Dick stared at her low cut huge breasts and winked her, the woman smiled proudly and just said, "Americano?".

"Si, senorita." Dick was in a hurry to meet Diana, he had no time to set any date since the day had just begun.

The woman left the bird cage swinging her hot butts hidden by her tight skirt.

"It's really fuckable!" Dick said to himself.

The elevator went up and stopped on the 7th floor at last.

Dicky stepped out of the three ways elevator and just met a Mexican security guard standing at the door side.

"Me permite, senor." The dark Embassy guard passed his electronic indicating sticker over Dicky's body.

"Pasa, por favor, senor.' The guard showed his smiling teeth.

The American private-eye approached the reception desk and asked for senorita Diana.

"Just a minute, please.' The slim young receptionist raised the tube and buttoned a number, she said some words in Spanish to the phone meanwhile she eyed Dicky to sit on the chair in front.

The negro guard appeared again and accompanied Dicky to go with him, after walking about a 5 meters distance corridor, they arrived a door closed on the right side of the corridor way.

Diana Martinez appeared behind her door, she invited Dick to sit on the chair face to her desk.

The pretty young lady dyed her hair to light brown, the elegant dark blue outfit highlighted her sexy shape, coffee red lips shine was outstanding her Latin sun burn tanned healthy skin.

"And what happened? Dicky." Diana sat straightly and cared her body against the high back executive chair.

"Oh, ... I'm here for the case No.705, you know the case, don't you?"

"Something to drink? Dicky. You like Mexican café?" Diana purposely touched her opened shirt button slightly.

"Yes, please." Dick's attention was almost attracted into Diana's breast cut division.

Diana dialed her desk phone button saying, "Dos café, por favor!"

"I'll give you the code number of the case No,705 and the key of the save box in the Citi Bank, you have to go and take the case on your behave. My order is limited right up to here, you know." Diana said smilingly.

"Well, I see." Dick extended his legs and tried to relax himself a bit.

A Mexican young girl pushed the door in and served two cups of Mexican coffee.

"You have been in B.A, many times, you know where the Citi Bank is?" Diana opened her desk drawer and drew out a prepared office file, she handed it to Dick over the desk.

Dick tasted the café and nodded the head.

"How about dinner for tonight?" Dick took advantage to invite Diana for a date.

"Tonight we have Embassy's reception in Hilton Hotel at 8 p.m. if you want, you could come just show my name." Diana softly refused Diana's Dicky's requesting.

"May be some other day, for old time's sake." Dicky covered skillfully his uncomfortable point.

"Sure, Dicky." Diana got up even officially, she saw Dicky off up to the office door.

Diana Martinez was the distant relative of current Mexican President, she went into the Foreign Ministry as young as 18 after she had finished her high school studying since her father Eduado Martinez was the Foreign Minister, she traveled several Latin American countries during her 7 years diplomatic career. Eduado Martinez left the Ministry two years ago and took the post of Secretary General of the Presidency, he is one of the favorite sons of the President, his daughter rapidly got professional diplomatic license and was chosen by Mexican Central Intelligence Agency as an international affair agent. She should combine her job with the U.S. CIA and FBI agencies, then Tompson appointed Diana to connect Dicky's mission.

Diana dialed her private cell phone and said to the person at the other side of the wire, "El hombre estuvo aca." Then she cut down the phone.

Dick Willians left the building gate and found that his rental car was out of order, then he waved to the first cab passing along the street, the cab stopped immediately and the driver opened rear door for him with his right hand extended.

He jumped in and just said, "Citi Bank Central." The old driver silently closed the door then switched the meter lazily, the car began to float into the car-pool of the peak rush hour.

It was a short distance, but the old driver took a long ride, he made Dick a 'tourist sightseeing'.

The 'Americano' arrived the Citi Bank's gate almost 20 minutes later.

He gave the old 'tachero' 15 Pesos then got off the car.

B.A.'s Citi Bank was located at the center of downtown's financial area, it was called 'B.A.'s Wall Street', this area consisted of a few blocks, San Martin and Sarmiento were the most popular corner where dozens local and foreign bank's head offices were concentrated around the area most exchange houses also put their main branches in the neighborhood of the zone.

Dick stepped up the classic marble made gateway and went down to the basement where the safe boxes were located.

The main clerk of the division accompanied him to the place, they put the twin keys together and opened the case. Dick eyed the clerk who asked excuse and left for a distance, Dick took out the main bag which attached an ink printed label written: 705.

It was a thick leather made bag, he carefully kept into his briefcase then walked out the insurance division.

Dicky held his briefcase and followed the stairway to go to the ground floor, the bank began to full in more clients and made the big hall look narrower.

He planned to go back first to the Hotel, then to think what to do? His briefcase was handcuffed to his own hand, he came out from the Citi Bank heading first to Corrientes Avenue, it was only one block distance from the Sarmientos corner, the sidewalk of San Martin street was narrow, he still recalled some main streets in B.A.'s downtown since his last trip was made in 1978 since the time hasn't change so much. He felt tired and exhausted. He took merely two minutes to reach the intersection,

People walking around like they did everyday in this big city, he jointed passenger's wave walking and appreciating the nice shopping window view.

A dark VW semi old car stopped by his side, two strong man got off the oil can and neared him slightly, they held Dick's both arms and pushed him into the rear seat of the car together with them, it happened so quickly that he had no time to realize what was really going on? The third strong man was sitting on the driver's seat. Dicky's eyes were bounded by a black adhesive belt that made him lost completely the sights.

"Listo?" he just heard the man on the driver's seat asked the two strong men who were sitting separately closed to his both aides.

"Si, listo. Jefe." They spoke Argentine Spanish.

He received strong strokes the both guys elbows who sat side by side with him liked a sandwich.

"Quieto, hermano, si te portas bien, no va pasar nada!" one of the short strong men said to him in a very law and hard voice.

Dick found himself pressed by gun points on both sides of his kidneys.

"I don't speak Spanish, please speak English, maybe you found the wrong man." Dick Williams said in his darkness.

"No hablamos English. You, Dick Williams, yes." The driver answered him in broken English.

"So, what you really want?" Dicky felt the car was speeding and running into a wide avenue, he calculate the time and the city-map he still kept in his memory, they might running on Avenida 9 de Julio heading to the direction to go to the south suburban area.

It was still hot rush hour, he was thinking how to get out of this mess.

The adhesive tape was so tight that obliged him to keep silence since he began to feel a little short breath.

After about 15 minutes ride, the car seemed yet had not plan to stop, Dicky was imaging the route they were taking, but that didn't last too much time, he felt a mere pain on his left neck, somebody gave him an injection.

"Shit, ..." He lost his conscience before he wanted to say something more.

The room was dark not because the day was getting later, but because the black cloth curtains that covered all the windows, it was terrible hot on the middle February of Argentina, a slow ceiling fan was circling lazily. Dicky found himself sitting on a wooden stool in front of a square table, his hands were free, the room was empty and nobody was present. A pocket of 'Jockey Club local cigarette and a glass of water were sat on the table quietly.

"Where's my briefcase?" he told to himself, that was all he got. Dicky put his hand into his trousers pocket, nothing was lost, including his personal wallet, his passport, credit cards, even 575 U.S. dollars cash and about 350 pesos.

"What they want was only his briefcase and the most important things, his secret bag: No.705."

He felt so thirst, his throat was burning, he took up the glass and drunk it out.

The cold water calmed him a little, then he took the cigarette pocket and drew out one king size and lit it with his made in Taiwan electronic lighter.

He got up and raised up one of the dark curtains, the strong sun light flew in, what he could see was green plain and field, the house was a wooden one, he easily opened the wooden door and let himself out of the jail.

"Shit!" he was sorry for his out of caution, it was a shame for an American private-eye.

His wrist watch pointed 2:30 p.m., he closed back the fucking door with his foot kick, a piece of letter paper size note fell down on the floor. Dicky picked it up and read it:

Mr. Dick Williams,

We need your brief case and please don't insist to find it back.
This is not your country, go back to America as soon as you can get the next plane. We owe you nothing and we will not hurt you if you leave the country in time.

Good luck!
My name is Deutch

Dick kept the paper into his jacket pocket.

The sun was hot, he could see the nearest highway was about 200 meters away, he decided to walk and first to reach the road.

"What a fucking morning, . . ." he complained to himself, after he had reached the road, he found the only one shop located lonely by the right side of the road.

The Café got no name, an iron plain written 'Coca Cola' was hanging on the entrance side.

He went in directly and sat on the first old wooden table he got.

An old man neared his table saying, "Buenos tardes, senor, que desea?"

Dick didn't raised his head and just said, "Coca Cola, por favor!" he used some few Spanish he had learned from his career.

The old man left and brought him a glass with ice, he put the glass on the table then opened skillfully the Coco Cola button cap and served a half into his glass then left silently.

Dicky drunk all to the button as if spring water he found in the desert.

"What a shit place is here?" he took out one more cigarette and went on thinking.

"Necesita algo mas? Senor." The old man approached him and said with questioning eyes.

"Donde estamos?" Dick answered him with a strange question.

"Estamos en la Argentina.' The old man looked at him puzzled

"Diga, como se llama este local?"

"Oh, estamos en Longchamp, 40 kilometros de Buenos Aires." The old man laughed innocently.

Dick took out his wallet and gave 10 pesos into the old man's hand.

"Muchas gracias, senor.'

Dicky got out of the Café.

He saw a payphone box in seeing distance, then he decided to make a phone call.

The suburban of Longchamp town was as old as 1930's American farm town, but luckily Telefonica Espana had installed B.A.'s city telephone networks. Middle class farmers obtained their advantage to have their private phone lines.

Dick inserted his telephone card and dialed directly to the Mexican Embassy.

He caught Martinez through her cellphone.

"What happened? Dicky. Where are you?" Diana answered quietly.

"I'm here in a small town called Longchamp, what a fucking place is here? I was kidnapped and three guys took away my briefcase included case No.705." Dick said loudly through the tube.

"O.K. be cool. Does anybody else know that?"

"No, I don't think so!" Dick said in a very upset tone.

"Good, now do me a favor, take a cab and go straightly to your hotel and

I'll be there around 4 p.m., right?"

Diana cut the phone as soon as she finished her words.

"Shit!" Dicky took out his card and caught the first cab, he went on saying,

"Corrientes y Parana, por favor."

The driver pulled down the Taxi meter excitedly began to run for his long distance fortune trip.

It was a great fucking business at this terrible business-slow period, nobody made one cent since over two years long economic depression.

"Vd. es Americano?" the driver put his radio aloud and intended to open the chatting box.

"Shut off your radio and bring me to that fucking place, you understand?"

Dick said very impatiently.

"Si, senor." The dark skinned driver got his sense only for reading his face.

The old oil can spent almost one hour for bring Dick back to Hotel Columbia.

He threw the money to the driver and went up to his room 202.

It was about 3;30 p.m.

He took the two ways elevator and easily arrive his room door.

He put his room key and pushed the door open.

The simple room was completely registered by somebody, the couch was down inside up, the closet and desk were opened.

But nothing was lost excepting his private note book, it was a leather flamed old book he had used for the last five years.

Dicky used to note all his events and date on his old book no matter it's order in time and places.

Dick sat on the bed edge for a short break, he raised the phone tube and advised the counter clerk to go up immediately.

Hotel Columbia's servicemen usually could handle simple broken Argentine English.

"We have to llamar policia." The chief waiter said to Dicky.

"Forget it, just bring me a glass of whisky double on the rocks, please."

His face was pale and tired.

"yes, sir. En seguida!" the water left down.

Dick lay on his back on the couch, he really didn't know how to do?

The waiter came back with Dick's room service order.

"Bring me one portion more, I'll get a company, let the lady in, her name is Diana."

"Yes, sir."

Diana arrived to the room 202 at about 4:15 p.m., she still wore the morning's suit and looked a little tired, she neared Dicky and pulled a chair to the bed side then sat beside Dicky.

"Tell me, what was really happened?"

Diana put her hand to arrange Dicky's messed hair and sealed gently her lips on Dicky's forehead.

"Make love with me, Diana. I'm so tired.'

Dick took the chance and hugged Diana's sexy body into his arms.

"No, please. Dicky. You need to get a rest. I've got to prepare everything for tonight's Embassy reception, it's near 5 p.m. now."

"I'm so tired, I need a relax." Dicky kissed her lips strongly.

Diana pushed him down, then got up quickly, she arranged her suit saying, "Look, you have to take a hot shower, then take a nap and come to Hotel Hilton at 8 p.m., I'll wait for you and we've got to talk, all right!"

The waiter knocked at the door and brought Dicky's room service order.

Diana signed the bill saying to the waiter.

"Take it back, don't disturb the gentleman until 8 p.m. and 20% tip for you on the account."

Diana closed the door, then left.

Dicky woke up about 5:30 p.m., he found himself still laid on hotel's bed, he bathed then changed a dark suit, after a short

15

nap, he felt rather better, he went down to the street and waved to a cab to go to Maipu street, he needed a long distance call Tompson.

He registered on the check-in counter of Telefonica Argentina's city office, the clerk sent him to the payphone booth No.27, he went into the booth and sat comfortably, he dialed DDI number directly to Mexico City, and fortunately he caught Tompson on the line.

Dick told the problem he met and waited for his chief's further indication.

"I knew everything already, Dicky. Diana have phoned me an hour ago, it was just a test for you, you are really a fucking bad private eye, the case file No.705 you've took out from the Citi Bank's save was a forged one.

Now, write down carefully the points, you got a pen with you? Boy." Tompson said quietly.

"Yes, chief." Dick felt himself like a cooked shit.

"Go to the address below tomorrow morning to meet Mr. Hopskin at San Jose 256, 10 piso. He will give the real case file no.705 and your expense fee, be careful, you are not in your right condition. Over."

Tompson cut the communication right off.

"Asshole, son of bitch!" Dicky insulted the tube, he got almost furious.

There was no choice, he paid the account and went out of the phone office.

Corrientes Avenue was again into the rush hour.

He stepped into a tailor shop, chose a smoking suit and a pair of good reception shoes, the ticket marked only 300 pesos

(U.S. dollars 100), it was a good fucking buy, no where in the earth could be found such a good price as in Argentina, the worse moment for this once ever been a rich country.

He went back to Columbia Hotel walking alone the avenue, he appreciated hundreds nice girls asses, the hottest and most sexy in the world.

The nice sunset street scene relaxed his bad mood.

"Go back to the hotel and then go to participate Diana's party."

He thought while he was walking along.

"You want to fuck my asshole, man. I only charge you 50 pesos." An English speaking young and tall guy neared Dicky and said to his ear.

'Go to fuck yourself with your middle finger! You asshole!"

"Shit! What a fucking bad day!"

Dicky almost got full up set.

B. As Hotel Hilton was located along the north river side, close to Retiro Railway Station and a huge park. An outstanding clock tower was a remarkable symbol of this area.

Retiro was also one of the cheap prostitute area in Buenos Aires except Plaza Once and Plaza Constitucion.

Hotel Plaza was just located 200 meters away at the end of Florida street and intersectioned Cordoba Avenue, the famous Plaza San Martin and Foreign Ministry palace were looking face to face one to the other. B.A. City never lost it's romantic flavor at any moment everywhere of the City.

Dick went back to his hotel room and dressed his new gala suit, he called the head waiter to prepare a Remis car for him ready to ride to Hotel Hilton.

The middle aged Remis driver opened the door for Dicky and hold it until he went into his back seat comfortably, the driver was rather professional, he put soft tango music along the ride.

The black BMW car took Corrientes Avenue up to Cerrito then turned to right to the corner of the Avenida de Mayo where National Congress House was located, the ride was quiet and peaceful. Dicky was relaxing and let the driver do what he wanted. The dark skin driver took Callao Avenue up to Santa Fe then slide straight down to the Plaza San Martin. There was a considerable slope connected with Plaza de San Martin and Avenida del Libertador where sited the elegant Hotel Hilton.

The car drove directly into the gateway.

"Thank you, sir." Dicky said to the elegant driver.

"De nada, senor. Y buenas noches."

One of the red cap approached the car door and opened it for Dicky.

Dicky took ten pesos note out, then put it into the boy's white glove covered hand.

The reception party was taking place on the ground hall, it was about 20:30.

The elegant salon was already full of guests.

Dicky shook hands with ambassador's couple who stood at the entrance of the party salon accompanied by two attaches.

Diana was walking around the guests, she greeted and kissed most of the VIPs.

A white coated waiter approached Dicky and let him choose the drinks on the tray, he took a glass of white wine.

"I was looking for you, Dicky. Why did you come so late." Diana appeared from nowhere.

She wore a dark summer evening long dress, high heeled silver color shoes, diamond like necklace, she looked really fucking beautiful and charm.

Dicky stared at her and was even momentarily seduced by her appearance.

"Come, I'd like to present you to a very important diplomat." Diana hooked Dicky's finger and let him walking among the guests.

"Mr. Lee, may I present you one of my best friends, Mr. Dick Williams, he's the federal agent of the U.S. government."

Diana showed Dick a tall and lean Chinese diplomat.

"How do you do? Mr. Williams. My name is James Lee, the security attaché of the Embassy of the People's Republic of China."

Dick William shook hands with the tall Chinaman meanwhile he was studying up to down his appearance. The ivory color face man was in his early forties, he wore a dark blue suit, gray silk tie, pure white silk shirt and a pair of 400 dollars Italy shoes.

"What a socialist country officer!" Dicky was thinking while he went on studying the man's face. He looked like a very educated gentleman excepting his pair of eagle eyes which were the mirror of his spirit window. Dick failed to look at him very straight.

"This is a secret agent man!" Dick got his sixth reaction from his rear brain.

"You both enjoy the party. I need to greet the couple of Canadian ambassador."

Diana left them alone after an excuse.

"This is my name card." Lee picked out a piece of white paper from his inside pocket and handed it to Dick Williams.

Charles Lee
3rd Class Secretary

Embassy of the People's Republic of China in Buenos Aires

"Oh, thank you." Dick Williams received it and read it over.

"Are you always be found in your office? Mr. Lee."

"You could contact me with my private number." Lee gave Dicky another private card, it was written:

Tony Liu
President
Lius International Trading S.R.L.
Av. Del Libertador 5555
Buenos Aires Capital Federal
Tel: 541-11-4886-7869 20-24 hrs.

"Are you also called Tomy Liu, Mr. Lee." Dicky stared at him with a smart smile.

"Only commercially, Mr. Williams.' He winked to Dicky.

"Oh, I see." Williams kept the two cards together into his side pocket.

"You want to have a word with me at the rear garden? Mr. Williams."

Lee moved his wine glass in his right hand.

"Sure."

Lee turned his body then heading to the rear garden of the party salon.

Dicky followed him passing through a lot of guests.

The open air garden was quiet and peaceful, only a few couples were chatting and dancing.

Charles Lee stopped by a flowers bar, he changed a glass of champagne, then raised his glass to Dicky.

"Cheer, and be success for our case!" he said to Dick with his penetrating looks.

"What case? Mr. Lee." Dick surprised his question.

"I know your case beforehand, Mr. Williams." Lee sipped his champagne wine.

"Son of bitch." Dick said in his mind.

"You have nothing to do with FBI, haven't you? Mr. Lee." Dick asked Charles Lee straightly.

"Of course not, Mr. Williams. I'm a federal agent of my own government, but you are not a federal agent of the U.S. government."

"I've got your file photos in my office records.'

"What do you want from me? Mr. Charles."

"Nothing, Mr. Dick. I just want to be your help." Charles approached a garden table then sat down on a chair, he raised his hand to invite Dicky to sit in front.

Dick did it.

"Look, the person you are going to find is not in Argentina. So, don't lose your time.' Charles put his glass on the garden table.

"Which person? I don't know what are you talking about?" Dick even felt a little angry.

"I will be waiting for you or your phone call tomorrow night. You will see, tomorrow. Now I have to go and it's very nice to see you. Mr. Williams, good night and good luck.'

Charles Lee gave the hand to Dick, then rose up and left the salon.

"What kind of shit is that?" Dick found himself looking like a full fool.

"Is this seat free? Gentleman.' A bird voice female was asking Dick just behind his shoulder.

"Oh, of course. Please be seated." He hurriedly got up and met a young lady standing beside him with smiling eyes.

She was a German like middle size elegant lady, a pair of dark blue eyes, reddish brown hair and her lips were painted in night rose color lip shine, her black evening dress covered tightly her sexy shaped body, a pair of silver combined diamond stones earrings called Dicky's attention.

The lady sat just opposite to Dicky softly, Dicky felt her light but rather evident fragrance floating around the air.

He was almost attracted by her charming appearance.

A red uniform waiter neared them and let them chose the drinks.

"Are you alone? Mister." the lady said to Dicky politely.

"My name is Dick Williams. I'm a CNN reporter in Buenos Aires, and may I have your name? lady.'

"Oh, really. My name is Christine Anderson. I'm the adviser of Mr. Gorge Brown, you sure know who he is?" the young lady was in her middle twenties, but she spoke in a very European accent English.

"Sure, I know George Brown. I had an interview with him last month, but not in Buenos Aires." Dick Williams felt that this party is surrounded by dozens of international spies.

"Did you? Mr. Williams. My uncle in law is a very kind man you know."

"Sure, he is. Miss Anderson.'

"Liar!" Christine said to herself.

"Where are you going after the party? Mr. Williams." Christain's eyes were full of charm.

"I decided to go back to my hotel. I got a tough day, you know. Miss Anderson."

"You don't live in a flat instead of living a hotel?"

"I used to live so, you see, lady. Our newsmen travel often."

"I believe so, Mr. Williams. I say, do you want to have a cup of tea with me in my flat, Mr. Williams. I am living alone and I'm interested to talk with you about some news items since my uncle's staff always needs enough media information, you know."

"Oh, with pleasure, miss Anderson.' Dick Williams felt rather tired, but this beauty's seduction was stronger than him.

"Then, let's go now." Anderson got up from the seat, her low cut evening dress was highlighting her pumped breasts.

"Now? Oh, I see." Dick Willaims got up in a hurry and followed Christian's steps toward the gateway.

"Hey, what's happened? Dicky, I've got words to talk with you." Diana Martinez ran after Dicky with a somehow suprising.

"I see you tomorrow, Diana.' Dicky waved his hand and left.

Christine Anderson drove her double seats white BMW sports running speedy along Avenida del Libertador, she put Dick to sit shoulder by shoulder with her.

Her ylang-ylang fragrance smoothly floating over on to Dicky's nose.

"Where are you going? Lady." Dicky questioned politely.

"To my house, as I've said. Don't worry, I am living alone." She gave him a big sweet smile under the summer moonlighting.

Buenos Aires northern up town always has her great charm if you really understand and had been living for a long time with her.

"Do you want a cigarette? Mr. Williams.'

"Oh, yes. Please." Dicky really wanted to take one.

Christan lit one from Marbollo Box for herself then passed the box to Dicky.

Dicky drew a piece of cigarette and lit it with his 'made in Taiwan' rather good quality European style lighter.

"I'm living in Martinez. Do You know the place? Mr. Williams."

"Yes, madam. I've been here for my very first time in the year 1978, I still have a great memory over this beautiful town." Dick inhaled the smoke while the BMW was flying along the wild avenue.

"I'm living thrse, because there almost lived all the foreign diplomats, you see."

"Yes, I see. lady."

"Please don't call me lady, miss, madam, just call me Christen, or just call me Criss." The beauty beside stared at him with a very seductive glances.

"It's a nice name, Criss.' Dicky looked straightly into her eyes passionately.

He was rather drunk but still remained his clear mind, he was not thinking sexually how to involve with this girl, but he really was falling into her seductions.

Christine handled her car like an experienced car runner, they reached

Olivo city limit in a very short time since they were chatting accompanied by the American pop music.

"It will be the second stop from here, right?" Dicky had a very fresh memory over north B.A.'s map.

He experienced once a long distance car persecution after one wanted international terrorist right on this avenue 26 years ago, the tough guy was under his arrest at last as far as Tigre, it's the city town on the extreme end of this road. Dicky was still very young, he fought with the middle aged Mexican native man and was hurt by the wanted man's knife on his belly and on his left leg, his body was fortunately cured two months later, CIA gave him a bronze medal and 5,000 U.S. dollars reward, it was a good sum of money in the States, but not in B.A.'s good time. The country was under the shadow of the so called 'dirty war', but the economy of the country was in her good fucking moment.

Dicky left B.A.'s German Hospital near October 1978 and went back to the States and since then he never came back again up to now.

This time he received Tonpson's order by accident, otherwise he'll never image that he would come back to Argentina anymore.

"What are you thinking? Mr. Williams."

Christine turned the car into the left side lane of Avenida del Libertador 14,500, it's right Martinez downtown.

"Oh, I just reached my former visiting of the city.'

"This is the place, Mr. Williams." Christine stopped her car along the residence of a huge luxurious residence.

A Carlos Gardel type dim classic street light was standing along the gateway.

The bushes and flower wall surrounded house was quiet and rather romantic at middle night.

Dicky Williams was invited to go into the house with Christine Anderson.

They passed the green bushes decorated gateway and walked toward door of the house.

It was a marble paved path connecting the copper made front door and the gate entrance.

Christine led Dicky to walk along the path, her sexy back figure just swimming in front of Dick's sights.

It was the first time Dicky got chance to study clearly Christine's charming figure, she was around 172 cm tall girl, slim, elegant, healthy and in rather sport like fashion.

He tight butts swimming while she was walking her elegant shoulder resembled a model's shapeliness, any macho man could not stand behind her without some sex imaginations.

"Here we are, Mr. Williams.' Christine inserted her door key and opened the living room door.

"After you, Lady." Williams stood after Christine politely.

"Thank you." Christine turned her head back and threw a charming smile to Dick.

The living room was huge, classic, peaceful, comfortable and modern installed like most of the luxurious residences were.

Dick was invited to sit on a long Loise XVI sofa, Christine closed the door then went into her bed room after asking an excuse.

The palace style ceiling lamp focused the huge room with soft blue dim light.

Dicky sat comfortably on the sofa and fell into his dreams without noticing himself.

Christine prepared two glasses of iced champagne on the table and sat quietly waiting for Dicky's wake,

She was dressed in a piece of transparent white summer robe nothing underneath.

Dicky opened his eyes after 5 minutes and found himself sitting just in front of a almost half naked beauty.

"You want a drink? Mr. Williams." Christine raised one of the glasses and handed it directly to Dicky.

Dicky received it and just looked at Christine sexy body.

"Cheer, Mr. Williams." Christine took the other glass then knocked it against Dicky's glass.

"Oh, yes, . . ." Dicky was tired and under somehow sexual desire, he raised his glass and drunk off the wine.

He felt some kind of giddiness, he fell again into his dreams.

Christine put her glass back on the tray, she got up, then walked slowly toward the table telephone.

"The guy is right here, boss!" Christine informed the man who was on the other end of the line.

Dick Williams found himself sat on a arm chair with both hands tied on the arms of it, his feet were also locked by a chain lock.

From the room where he sat was completely different than Christine's, the wall clock pointed 4:30 a.m.

A middle aged man in his light gray summer suit was sitting in front of him, his face was quiet and gentle, a glass of whisky was held in his left hand while his right hand was lighting a cigar which was sticking between his lips.

Dicky opened his eyes and just realized he was cheated by that beauty, he sighed but he really got no choice.

"Hello, Mr. Williams. Welcome to our club, my name is Tracy Dickson, I'm under an order to take care of you as soon as you could answered a question, I hope it will not cause a problem for you?" Dickson sipped his whisky.

"Where am I and what hell to do you and me?" Dicky felt furious and didn't know what was really happening?"

"This thing is very simple, what we want to know is that, what hell are you going to do in this country? Are you alone in this trip or you are planning something with an organized group?" the light suit man made comfortable his sitting position.

"Can you free my hands and feet?" Dicky was hot, nervous and under psychologically depressed.

"Nicky!" Dickson called aloud to the room next to the door.

A big and tall guy about 187cm came out as soon as he heard the order.

"Yes, boss."

"Make Mr. William comfortable, please."

"Sure, sir."

"His name is Nicky, he's my man, a nice guy." Dickson explained.

Nicky released Dicky's ropes skillfully.

"You want a drink?" Dickson inhaled mouthful his cigar while asking Dicky with his sights.

"No, thank you, you didn't answer my question yet?" Dick said coldly.

"We are in someplace of the B.A. city, you have not to worry about it, you will be taken back to your hotel room as soon as we'll get your answer." Dickson showed up one of his hand.

"I'm here like a tourist.'

"We know everything about you, buddy. Please don't make things complicated, you are a wise guy, what we want is very simple, you have to cooperate with us."

"I have nothing to do with you since I don't know exactly who you are and why you still hold me here? You have any legal right over me?" Dicky got a little quieter.

"I am the district chief of the SIDE, I have my full right to bother you for a very short time, you have broken the law if just as you said you're a simple tourist.'

"May I see your I.D.? sir.' Dicky required the stranger's legal license.

"Anybody could have a false document." Dicky added.

"Nicky!" Diskson called Nicky again.

"Show Mr. Williams our I.D.!" Dickson made a dry smile.

Nicky approached Dicky just raised his both fits and made Dicky two black eyes without any previous notice.

Dicky felt heavy hot pain and a full head of golden stars.

He made a deep long breath, then took out his handkerchief to tear out his mere blood which was dropping out slowly from his lip angular.

"Call No. 222-541-9068 and ask Mr. Tompson, that's all I can say."

"You have to tell me this at the very first moment, man.' Dickson laughed dirty.

He went to the room next then went back about 5 minutes later, he called Nicky again then eared something to him, Dicky just nodded his head.

"Good morning, Mr. Williams. It's very nice to know you." Dickson said to Dicky then left off.

"Mr. Williams, I would bother you to use this again, we are going home.' Nicky covered Dick Williams eyes with the black belt.

Dicky was accompanied by two silence men, they took him outside the house, then put him into a car truck and closed it.

Dick Williams felt the car run on a country road quietly, it was a rather long ride, he could feel was the darkness and the sound of the car motor.

Dick counted more or less the time he had past on road, about 40 minutes later, he was taken out by the same men, they threw him directly on the roadside earth floor, then drove the car left.

Dicky's hands were free, he took off his cloth belt which covered his sights during the whole trip.

His watch showed the time, it was about 7:10 a.m., the field where he was thrown down was quiet and isolated.

He didn't lose anything, he got up slowly and intended to walk toward an ESSO gasoline filling station which was located about 100 meters away from the place.

He found a 24 hrs shop attached ESSO station, the first thing he did was to have a morning café.

The bartender greeting him from the other side of the counter.

"Café con leche, por favor." Dicky was tired even exhausted.

The fat man served the morning café quickly.

"Donde estamos? senor" Dick asked the old bartender.

"Aca es City Bell, estamos en el sur de Buenos Aires." The old man answered.

"Shit." Dick Williams got no choice and began to take his breakfast.

He put ten pesos on the counter and was ready to walk out to the street.

"Keep the change!" Dick walked straight toward the door.

"Gracias." The fat old man said in aloud voice.

Dick Williams took a cab and went back to Hotel Columbia, it was about 10:10 a.m.

"What a fucking night and morning!" he murmured to himself.

What he wanted was to take a shower and to have a long sleep.

The door was knocked.

"Who is it?" Dick answered on his back on the couch.

"It's me, waiter Roberto. May I come in?"

"Come in and tell me what do you want?"

"Mr. Williams, I saw you passed the lobby and looked rather tired, you have a tough night, haven't you?"

"I just want to ask you if you need a girl to accompany you, you know we have nice Argentine girl." Roberto went on, he used his hands drawing a woman figure in the air.

"Go to fuck yourself and please don't bother me any longer."

"Shit!" Dicky closed his eyes and intended to go on sleeping.

"Si, senor." Roberto closed the door and left off.

The telephone rang around 13:30 on Dicky's bed table.

Dick reached the table lazily and answered.

"Yes . . . ?"

"It's me Diana Martinez, is that you Dick? I was looking for you during the whole night, what hell were you staying? Is that reddish hair girl good? You left the party without saying hello to me? Are you all right?" Diana seemed very concerned about his 'well being'.

"I'm fine now. Could you come here right now? I have some words I want to talk with you." Dick cut the phone and could not continue his nap.

"What a hell I am living and what a mess I am involving?" he felt really bad and unhappy.

He got up slowly and put his clean suit.

The phone rang again and Roberto was asking Dick if he wanted a room service for his breakfast.

"Bring me a glass of red wine and a sandwich 'jamon y queso'." He cut the line off.

Roberto made quickly his room service for Dicky.

He drunk the full glass of red wine and ate out the fucking sandwich.

Dick William phoned the rental car agency and informed them that the fucking car was out of order, he wanted his money full refunded.

"Yes, we can give your money back but you have to pay your traffic fine and the cost we will spend to withdraw our car which is still parking as you said on Avenida de Mayo, if the car is still in there, you know Buenos Aires's car robbers are very quick and smart. If we can not find our car back, then Mr. Williams you have to pay our car in full value back." The clerk attended Dick's call very politely in his Argentine broken English.

"I'll pay you nothing, you gave me an old oil can and wasted my time and caused my great trouble, I'll send my lawyer to talk with you! Shit.' Dicky cut the phone off.

Diana Martinez knocked the door then pushed it in.

She wore a white suit and red semi high heels shoes, her dark sunglasses highlighted her charming red lips.

Dick Williams sat on the single sofa in the suite living room, he just gestured Diana to sit on the sofa opposite him.

"Tell me, what has really happened?"

Diana put her wide and ripped sexy ass on the sofa and while she threw her red purse on the third sofa on her left side.

"Even I don't know anything what has really happened?" Dick said like a defected dog.

"I was kidnapped again but what they wanted was only some information, then I sent them to call that fucking Tompson, and they released me after two hours integration, that's all.' Dicky recalled the main points of the details.

Diana listened, she didn't say anything special.

"You have got your file No.705, haven't you?"

"I don't. why?"

"No, I just ask you." Diana covered her expression.

"You remember who was the main man who had talked with you while they were holding you during the time?"

"A guy named himself Dickson, he certified himself as a district chief of SIDE."

Diana dialed her cellphone and made connection with somebody.

"Cacho, vos saber si hay un tipo que se llamar Dickson en vuestro districto?

Dicky heard unclearly the person called Cacho was speaking inside the phone.

"We can't find any Dickson who are working in any part of the SIDE network."

Daian concluded her conversations with Cacho then said to Dicky.

"Look, Dicky. I have to go back to my office and probably I've got to travel with my boss back to Mexico City 21 p.m., Anything you need, you could talk with my roommate, she is a close friend mine and she is also an agent working with the U.N.'s agency in Buenos Aires. Her name is Jane Cliton, don't worry, she is nothing to do with Bill Cliton, but I can tell you, she is a nice beautiful girl and she is in condition to assistant you during my absence, O.K.?" Diana wrote down the phone number on a paper slip and passed it to Dicky.

Dicky received the slip and put it inside his pocket.

"Then I have to see you again the coming week."

"I see you. Dicky." Diana neared Dicky and gave him a big kiss.

After Diana's left, Dicky fell into his loneliness again.

Dick Williams phoned Hopkins and sat an appointment at 15:00, he called a cab heading to San Jose 256, 10 piso where was the main office as Tompson indicated him through the phone yesterday.

The cab took Corrientes avenue down to the seaside direction up to Uruguary street then turned right to reach Avenida de Mayo 1400, the driver lazily floating on the route then stopped the car just along the pavement of San Jose 256.

It was an old Spanish style building, Dick Williams got off the car then paid the cab through the front car window, he studied few seconds before he got into the house. The 11 stories house functioned two ways classic elevators, he walked in along the dark but clean marble paved corridor up to the elevator doors.

He pressed the button then waited by the door side, San Jose was a quiet classic street like most cross streets around Avenida de Mayo present somehow a kind of classic European fashion, the elevator arrived after about 20 seconds, he stepped in, there was nobody except himself, he pressed his middle finger on the No.10 button, the old elevator took him slowly up, it took about another 20 seconds, the bird cage stopped again, he opened the door then got off from the cage.

There was a dark corridor in front of the cage's exit, he began to find one by one the places where were the names and titles corresponding apartment's owner.

Dick Williams walked along the corridor, there was nobody on the pathway, the dim ceiling light was not enough to identify the correct names of each unit of the floor.

He read over all the door plates, no any plate was written something about 'Hopskins', then he started to knock the door one by one in order to find Mr. Hopskins. The No.1 flat was nobody in, the second one was luckily answered, a young woman in her later twenties opened the door, her appearance was typical Latin American face, semi dark skin, big breasts and wide hips, she ware a red full cotton T-shirt and a fade color jeans, so tight and so hot, it underlined her harvest hot box as others street girls did.

"Excuse me, miss, could you tell me if Mr. Hopkins lives here?" Dick Williams asked her politely as soon as she put her long hair head outside the flat door.

"Oh, Americano, you want 'fucky, fucky!', 50 pesos.' The fat girl made him a hooker's smile.

"Shit!" Dick left her and turned to No.3 apartment.

There was an evident classic electric bell installed beside the right side of the door and luckily he found a small letter 'H' was painted just beside the bell.

He pressed the bell three times.

There was no body to answer, he waited and waited, at last he heard heavy steps approaching the door.

The door was opened, a very tall man, so tall as 190cm, thin and weak, in his early sixties appeared by the entrance of the door.

The man wore a semi new classic summer suit, light blue shirt, his old moccasin shoes were like most of the common people in the street, his touch like bright eyes studying Dick Williams from his feet up to the head.

"Are you Mr. Dick Williams?" the man opened his mouth.

Mr. Hopskin?" Dick Williams's mood changed, he was almost upset.

"Please come in." the man opened widely the door.

Dicky stepped in, Hopskins showed his way in.

He led Dick to pass the long corridor and arriving a rear room located at the end of the corridor, the both sides of the corridor were all office like rooms, the door were all closed.

Hopskins opened the room door then invited Dicky to go in.

It was a narrow but very private office room, a simple desk and two chairs. Hopskins went in and sat on an old leather armchair, hepointed to the chair opposite him to Dicky.

"Sit down, Mr. Dick Williams. Please."

A made in Taiwan mini computer was installed on the desk.

Dick Williams sat down as Hopskins said.

The silence man took out a leather jacketed file from the desk drawer, he opened it, then showed a book size color picture to Dicky.

"Do you know this man? Mr. Williams."

The person on the picture was a handsome oriental man in his early thirties, he ware a dark gray suit, white shirt and a reddish tie.

His eyes had somehow a gentle but smart sights, well cut gentleman hairdo, his staring expression was quiet and thoughtful, broad shoulder and elegant neck.

"I don't think so, Mr. Hopskin." Dick made comfortable his legs and answered affirmatively.

"And this girl, have you ever seen her once?" Hopskin showed Dicky the second photography.

"If you excuse me?" Dick upright his sitting position and took the picture down in his hand, he studied a few seconds, then threw it back on the desk.

"I've seen her right last night, her name is Christine Anderson.'

"Are you sure? Mr. Dick Williams." Hopskin stared at Dicky with very special looks.

"Of course, I'm sure.' Dicky smiled coldly.

"I could find her ever she turned herself in dust."

"You are wrong, Mr. Williams. Even we still don't know her true name, neither we can be sure she is still in Argentina now." He stopped a second, then went on, "What I want you to do is that, to find the Chinaman out, his true name, where he exactly is? And what is he really doing?'

"Why we have to find him? If you even know well his name and his background?"

"That's a very good question, the only data I can give you is that this guy is very very important to us. We have to catch him before he could make something bad." Hopshins put the picture back into the file, then pushed it to Dick's side.

"This is file No.705, it's all yours, Mr. William. You have you new passport and bank account number, both are here in Buenos Aires and a Swiss account, you have your VISA's golden credit card and the information we have collected in PC's disc. You have to check out of your hotel and move into the indicated flat in North B.A., the flat key is already kept into the file, you have not to return to Hotel Columbia any more, we will send a man to clean your account, the only person you have to contact is me."

"Don't come here anymore, my phone number in B.A. is written into the file, my code name from now on is Mr. Dutchman and don't call Mr. Tompson by phone anymore, he is out of the case from this moment.

Any question? Mr. Williams?"

Dicky received the new leather file then kept it into his briefcase.

"Do you know a guy named Charles Lee or Tomy Liu? Mr. Hopskin?" Dicky remained the person who had talked to him during the party.

"Call me Mr. Dutchman." He said seriously, then said, "Any person around you could presented you a forged name or I.D., so, you have to find an answer."

Mr. Dutchman got up from his chair as soon as he finished the words.

Dick Williams quitted Dutchman and left the flat, it was already 4:40 p.m.

He went out of the building, walked a few blocks up to Avenida de Mayo, he chose a street side café then went in and sat down by a very private table.

The waiter neared him, Dicky just showed him with the fingers, "an express coffee'.

He opened his briefcase and found his new flat address and the key.

He wrote down the place, then kept the key into his jacket pocket.

Dick Williams went out from the café, waved to a cab, he said the new address to the driver.

"Quelmes 45oo." He said to the cab driver.

It was a long city tour from San Jose to Quelmes street specially into the second rush hours.

The B.A.'s taxi drivers never hurry up, they take a passenger then began to show the city for the clients especially for 'street-stranger' or a foreign passenger.

The driver who took Dick Williams was a typical 'Argentina Chanta', he was a Spanish and Italian original mixed semi-white skin person, middle age, pumped belly, big nose and wore a heavy mustache like most Latin men do.

They are kind but sly, self considered smart but really carry not high class brain, they like make joke if you can speak fluent Spanish and could understand well B.A.'s local fashion slang.

Dick's driver intended to speak with him but North American broken Spanish and Argentine fragile Spanishized English could not meet at the end, the ride was rather heavy since nobody could understand one the other.

Dick was felling into the mysterious of file No. 705, his mind was dipping into the some special points during the way, he didn't even pay any attention to the street scene.

The chanta driver thought that if I could not earn more money from this ride, I could not earn today's bread, then he made his claver decision, he turned the cab first directly to the plaza constitution, the famous bus and railway terminal of B.A., it took about 30 minutes, then he drove up the car heading to Plaza Retiro, after that, he took a big U-turn, then drove on to the celebrated Avenida del Libertador up to Belgrano area, where located new established B.A.'s Chinatown since most of the Chinks were living around. The rush hour took him another 40 minutes, the driver skillfully only chose red traffic lights for stopping on, the taxi meter ran and pesos ran too. Dick Williams didn't pay any attention, anyway, U.S. government will pay the traffic fare, threw some bucks for this poor Argentine driver was not a matter, anyway, he needed to support his fucking family as well.

"Ya eatamos, senor." The driver raised his excited smile, the meter read 87 pesos, it almost worthed for three days earning for his job. Dick William gave him a 100 pesos note, then patted his shoulder saying,

"Keep the change."

"Tanchu Mary Mooch! Senor.' The driver was very proud of his 'road map' truck.

Quemes was a parallel street to Santa Fe Avenue, they almost go in the same level of the numbers, so Quemes 4500 was just one black distance from Santa Fe 4500.

Dick Williams went off the car then headed directing to the address indicated into the file.

Quemes 4525 was a nice residential building located at the next door of a private clinic.

He inserted the gate door key into the key hole and opened the gate door, a red carpeted long corridor connecting the entrance and the two elevators.

He went directly to the flat No.705, it was a two bed rooms nice flat, nice living room combined a small dining room, a studying room, bathroom and a kitchen.

He sat first on the living sofa, threw his file case aside, raised his feet on a matching chair, lit a Jockey Club king size cigarette, the dim light and remote controlled sweet music made him temporary relaxed himself for a while.

He really needed a short nap after those two fucking days.

Dick Williams lay on the sofa chair, quickly fell into the sleep.

It was about 10 p.m. when Dicky woke up, he went to the kitchen refrigerator took a bottle of white wine and a soda gas, he put enough ice cubic then poured about one half glass of the wine into the glass, then a perfect cold drink was made. You can buy any fine white and red wine in any place of Argentina and to be sure nobody will cheat you, wine in this country is already a part of culture.

Dicky went on reading the file.

He took out the Chinaman's picture out of the file and began to study closely the image of person.

He recalled Mr. Hopkins's words, ...

Why the guy didn't want to tell him what was the name of this person?

. . . .

And why Mr. Hopkins didn't want to recognize Christine Anderson's identification?

He returned his memory back to the past 48 hours.

Diana Martinez and so called 'Charles Lee' were two persons still 'real' up to now.

Dick raised his phone tube, then dialed the number Charles Lee gave him, according to Lee, he should be called as 'Tomy Liu' after 20:00 hours. He marked the number, the phone was attended after 3 to 4 ringers.

"Mr. Tomy Liu?"

"Is me, who is calling please?" Dicky heard the voice of Charles Lee, he was sure the number was not wrong.

"This is Dick Williams speaking, do you remember the Hilton's night party?"

"Of course, I remember you. Mr. Dicky, I'd like to invite you here for a couple of drinks, I have very important things want to talk with you, you know my address? Don't you?"

"Your place is not far from mine, how about 11 o.clock?, you just take a cab and it only will take you ten more minutes.'

"Okey, Mr. Tomy, I think I will be there."

"Dicky hung the phone tube and just thought, "Why the guy already know where I live now? How strange."

"Let me first see what happens.' Dicky said to himself meanwhile he put on a summer coat and went out to the street.

His flat was only one block from Plaza de Italia, he waved to a cab and indicated Tomy's address.

The place Dicky was living belonged to the vicinity of so called 'Barrio Norte', from there began the extension of B.A.

City's middle class even richer people's residences as far as Tigre county.

The night was quieter than the day, Dicky reached Tomy Liu's place about 10 minutes later.

The two stories residence-like building was rather big and independent, it stood along the avenue, it was so remarkable one could confuse it as an embassy but a trading company.

Dick Williams got off the cab, heading directly to the gateway, an Argentine native security guard approached Dicky and requested his name, then he went back to the booth and asked through the phone.

Dick Williams felt quite uncomfortable for having to wait so long.

The dark guard came back with a smile and saying, "Pasa, por favor, senor Williams. Senor Liu esta esperando."

Dick followed his gesture heading to the building's doorway.

"Welcome, Mr. Williams. Please come in." Tomy Liu had already waited for him by the entrance accompanied by his aide, a middle aged silence man in his early fifties.

They led Dick to the living room after passing a long corridor paved by dark green carpet.

The big living was decorated in full Chinese communist fashion, a big size Mao Tse Tung's picture was hanging on the background of the wide room.

Dick was arranged to sit on a sofa just opposite to Tomy Liu, the silence aide just sat behind Liu.

"May I call you Charles, Mr. Lee? I am not used to address the same person in two different names." Dick said to Tomy Liu.

"I prefer you call me Tomy while we are staying in this house. Maybe you will consider it as an impolite manner, but please forgive me, Mr. Williams, it's our rule."

Dick didn't insist more.

"Tell me, Mr. Williams, what's your nature to visit me tonight?" Tomy Liu asked Dicky meanwhile he directed a male servant to serve Chinese green tea.

"What I want to know is that, you had told me the other night party, the man you are looking for is not in Argentina, what was the man you refered to? Mr. Tomy."

"You have to know better than me since you are in charge of the case." Tomy smiled smartly.

"I really not exactly know who was the man you refer to, could you give me any idea of that man?"

"He is a Chinese." Tomy took out his pipe and lit it.

"I know the man is a Chinese."

"A very important Chinese man.'

"And then, . . ." Williams was waiting for more information.

"You have not to insist to find him, because it's very dangerous for you."

"Mr. Tomy, may I know what's the real work you are doing in this office?"

"We are a trading company, a very practical one.'

"But you told me, you're the security attaché of the PRC's Embassy.'

"It's true."

"Was the man get something to do with the Embassy?"

"Not exactly." Tomy said.

"What will happen if I insist to find the man in Argentina?"

"I had told you, the man is not in Argentina."

"Mr. Williams." Tomy added, "Would you mind to go with me into the inner room, I think I've got something very interesting for you."

"I'd love to.'

"Good, then, please follow me." Tomy got up and heading to the inside part of the living, Dicky followed him.

The silent man didn't move from his place.

The inner room was a conference room like place not enough big but enough for six persons to make a meeting.

Tomy invite Dicky to sit on one of the seats, then he sat closely to Dicky.

"Look, we are only two in this room, nobody will hear anything except us. I'm the president of this company and I have my full capacity to represent the government of the People's Republic of China. I could offer you 5 million U.S. dollars if you just retire from this case, you know the sum of the money is enough for you for rest of your life, why don't you just write the final report and abundant this case, I could give you right now the half of the money, you just put your initial, right on this contract, it's so simple and the money is so hot. Be a wise guy, you could lose the great opportunity forever. So, Mr. Williams, this is my word, you could trust me.'

"You could give me five million bucks if I give up the case?"

"That's it." Tomy said with his secret smile.

"Is our conversation be wired?"

"100% confidential, Mr. Williams." Tomy put very serious face.

"I am an U.S. federal agent. I can't against my own rule, Mr. Tomy."

"Never mind, keep your time and think it over." Tomy Liu got up from his seat and ready to leave,

Dick Williams rose from the seat, he gave his hand to Tomy.

"So, you've made your decision."

"I didn't say that. Mr. Liu."

"I'll be waiting for your answer anytime since now, but please remember my words.'

Tomy accompanied Dick to the front door way.

"It's very nice to see you, Mr. Williams. You could find me here 20 to 24 hours from Monday to Saturday."

Dicky left the mansion, caught a cab and then headed to his new flat.

Dick Williams went into the building with the key, the elevator had nobody except himself, "The building is so quiet and almost in 'dead silence.' He told his mind while the bird cage was elevating.

He found his flat door under the dim corridor lights.

He put the key in, but surprisingly, it unlocked alone, that made Dicky raised his attention from the back waist, his breath turned to short. "Somebody must be inside." A sudden thoughts waved over his mind.

The ceiling light was on, since he had switched off all the lights before his leaving.

He pointed his gun ready for any bulk while he decided to move in at a very fast manner. "I have to catch this son of bitch." He made up his mind but no body was in the living neither any part of the rest rooms.

"Shit!" Dick sat on the living sofa, "Nothing was lost.", it was strange, "Somebody had been here.', he sat for a while, then went to the refrigerator and found a Brazil made beer 'Barhama', strong and very brazil-like.

He remoted his 20" color TV, it was a semi-new HITACHI, the new program was discussing how to solve the bank-frozen problem of the country and how was the trial processing of the hot news: A mysterious death of a stock market dealer who was suspected to be killed by her own family, a multimillionaire of the City.

Dick changed his cable channels to some U.S. movies and sports news, the beer and tiredness made him fell into the dreams.

It was 3:50 a.m. the morning next when Dicky opened his eyes, he found himself led on the same living sofa.

He reopened the file No.705, he read over page by page again and again.

'To find the unknown man out in any price.' was the real subject.

"This guy is priceless, then 5 million dollars is a shit!" Dick made his mind rather clean.

He kept the file into the safe, then went up to the john for a hot bath, he felt rather better after that.

The telephone rang.

Dicky run out of bathroom naked and caught the tube.

"Are you there? Dicky. It's me, Diana Martinez, I'm here in Mexico City I'm calling to see if you are all right?"

"Oh, it's you, Diana. Are you really in Mexico City? Yes, I'm fine, look, I want you to know one thing, the guy you presented me in the party, Charles Lee, is he a real diplomat? Can you tell me something more about him? I need the information." Diicky answered the phone on a single sofa chair.

"I know every diplomat in the party, but I know nothing in details about them, you know everybody is working for their country, you understand me?"

"So, you are working for your country too."

"Sure, Dicky, it's why I am working for the Mexico Embassy."

"You know Chinaman in B.A.? I mean, a very important Chinaman."

"Why don't you go to check in Chinatown or go to see Taiwanese Embassy.'

"Where is the Chinatown?"

"Ask any taxi driver, Dicky."

"Are you alone now in your room? Diana."

"Yes, I'm alone, why?"

"Nothing, Diana. I just want to know if you are living with a man?"

"It's my business, I like Mexico macho man, of course, but not now, I'm quite busy by my way, Did you visit Jean Cliton?"

"Not yet, Diana. I'll call her if it will be necessary."

"Good, be a good boy, one more thing, have you found anything strange in your flat?"

"Yes, why did you ask me this and how did you get my private phone number?"

"I have to take care of you, Dicky. I'll call you soon.'

The phone was cut off.

"Who is this fucking bitch?" Dicky hung the tube and kept on thinking.

Jean Clinton got up early, about 6 a.m., she was exercise her Tai Chi Fist learned from the Chinese Temple 20 blocks away, this seemed to let her feel enough relaxed after about 20 minutes moving. She was taking the work daily on her fifth floor's balcony facing the beautiful costal line of Rio de la Plata.

B.A. is not a charming and beautiful city except her current economic crisis. But for Jean Clinton, a jetsetter living on upper level society, she didn't feel anything which is effect her daily life.

She owned her private luxurious flat located on one of the most expensive area of B.A. City and she was a woman CEO of an international news agency branched in Argentina and directly related to the UN headquarter in Argentina. Her 350,000 U.S. dollars flat and a classic white Lincon sports car showed her economic and social entity for her behave.

The 27 years old reddish hair English origin beauty reached enough high comparing her youth.

Her 175cm slim and elegant shape accompanied her Harvard MBA degree made her stable leadership among her 12 employees.

North America Agency(NAA) located it's head office on the 3rd and 4th floors of the same building where was living Jean Clinton.

Jean took her simple continental breakfast at 7 a.m. on her white American style dinning table, her private maid Lusy served everything by the table as her daily work.

She began to read her Internet news around the world, open her E-mail box in her notebook PC, then she switched on the CNN channel to review the current hot lines.

After that, she took off her clothes to enjoy a morning hot shower bath in the bathroom next her huge living room.

Telephone rang, ten minutes after.

"Answer the phone, Lusy." Jean Clinton called aloud to her maid.

"Hola . . . ," Lucy answered in Spanish.

"Good morning, lady. I'd like to speak to miss Jean Clinton, please."

"De parte de quien?"

"This is Mr. Dick Williams speaking, I'm a friend of miss Diana Martinez."

"Un momento, por favor."

Lucy left the phone on the table and went to inform her mistress.

"Pass me to my line here." Jean Clinton took out her branch phone just by the wall closed to her bath tub.

"This is miss Jean Clinton speaking."

"Oh, excuse me, lady. My name is Dick Williams, I'm the regional reporter of the CNN, miss Diana Martinez asked me to call you for a private interview, and . . ."

"Oh, Mr. Dick Williams, Diana had mentioned your name to me a short while before, of course, take the liberty to visit my agency, you know my address, don't you?"

"Yes, lady, but I am not sure when will be the exact time for your convenience?'

"Come to my office if you like, 10 p.m. is that all right?"

"Sure, lady. I'll be there on time.'

"Okay, then I'll see you at 10 a.m."

Jean Clinton hung the phone and went on with her bathing.

Dick Williams got off from the yellow and black combined taxi and found himself standing on the Avenida del Libertardor 7000, he paid the tachelo and easily found the building a few steps away where was located Jean Clinton's head office.

It was a hot summer day, Buenos Aires was in her traditional holiday season, but this year's vocation wave seemed decreasing quite bit.

He stepped on the full glass doorway and headed to the four ways elevators.

The silver plate on the wall behind the security counter titled Jean Clinton's firm name, the dark skinned province face security guard showed him the 4th floor after Dick Williams announced the person he wanted to see.

The guard accompanied politely to the door then pressed the button for him.

The speedy modern bird cage took Dicky up to the forth floor within few seconds of time.

The door opened, a sky blue summer clothes uniformed young girl received him with a charming smile.

"Welcome, Mr. Dick Williams. Please follow me, our CEO is expecting you at her office.'

"What a hot bitch!" Dicky said to himself while he stepped after the tight but riped ass of the hot sexy Argentine girl.

"Yes, lady.' Dicky answered politely.

Jean Clinton sat on her executive chair in her luxury and elegant CEO office.

Dicky followed the receptionist and imaging how will be Jean Clinton's appearance,

The girl pulled open Jean's office and gestured Dicky to go in.

"Come in, Mr. Williams, I'm welcoming you as the name of North America Agency." Jean Clinton stood up behind her wide desk and showed the chair opposite her with her charming blue eyes inviting Dicky to sit on.

"How do you do? Miss Clinton, I'm very pleased to meet you."

"The pleasure is mine, Mr. Williams." Jean Clinton studied up to down Dicky's appearance.

The same girl went in and served both American coffee.

"Diana called me and mentioned Mr. Williams. I would like to know what could I help you?"

"Oh, yes, I'm here since I know that you're the close friend of Diana." Dicky studied the British like beauty in front of him, but he didn't answer exactly the question.

"I think so, Mr. Williams, as I know, you are in charge of an important case."

"Something like that."

"So, tell me straight, what is exactly you want to know?" Jean Clinton said in a very sharp and still manner.

"Do you know this man? Miss Clinton." Dicky took out the picture of the Chinaman right from his inner pocket and showed it to Jean.

"I don't think so, Mr. Williams. Why don't you go to Chinatown and ask somebody maybe they know well their society here." Jean's face moved merely.

Dicky noticed her expression.

"Would you present me someone in Chinatown if you know somebody there?"

Jean Clinton opened the drawer and took out a paper slip, she wrote down a name and the address.

"Go to see this man, maybe he could help you, that's all I can do, Mr. Williams." Jean Clinton rose from the chair, she showed her pride and elegant shape.

Dicky recived the paper and left the office room.

He headed to one of the elevators entrance, the receptionist ran after him saying, "Mr. Williams, our CEO asked me to give you her name card and this key, it's for one of her cars, you would go tonight to the saying address and for the car, miss Clinton decided to rent for you free for the time you would stay in Buenos Aires.

Dicky received the card and the key, he felt rather puzzled.

The elevator just arrived, he took it and said goodbye to the girl.

He went to a coffee shop nearby after he left the building.

Dicky chose the open air table on the wide sidewalk, a young waiter neared him, he ordered an express coffee and a piece of Ricota cake.

The first paper slip was written:

MONK SHIH LIN
FU KONG TEMPLE
MONTANESE 2100
BS. AIRES
TEL: 4778-9827

The second card written in English artistic letters:

Jean Margereter Clinton
Blue Star Agency
Automobiles Buy & Sell
Av. Del Libertador 14,500
Martinez, Pica. Bs. Aires

Dicky raised his cellphone and marked directly 4778-9827.

"Hola, . . ." an Chinese accent middle aged voice answered the phone.

"I would like to talk to Monk Shih Lin?" Dicky said in polite English.

The phone was cut down.

Dicky redialed the number.

"Hello . . . ," a foreign accent European like woman answered the phone.

"Good morning, lady. I would like to speak to Monk Shih Lin."

"Oh, he is out of the office now, who is speaking?'

"My name is Dick Williams, an American reporter, Miss Jean Clinton gave me the phone number and I would like to make an interview appointment with monk Shih Lin about some Buddhist subjects."

"Oh, it's okay. Please just wait for a moment, . . ." the woman left the tube and left the room.

Dicky held the phone and waited for a response, the minutes passed, but the phone was dead."

"Fucking monk and fucking nun." Dicky felt a little anger.

He closed the phone and went on eating his cake.

Dicky decided to go to the place personally without any previous advice.

He finished the snack and paid the bill.

It was 11:45 a.m., he waved to a cab and headed directly to the place.

Twenty blocks were short for a cab ride, he reached the temple in five minutes.

The building was simple constructed.

The street was silent and the red temple door was closed like a seal.

He found the door bell at last.

The door was opened after about 5 minutes waiting.

"Si, senor?" a young man in his early thirties stood by the entrance way, his right hand raised in Buddhist sign.

"I would like to see monk Shih Lin!" Dick answered in English.

The young man wore Buddhist like Chinese summer suit, seemed to understand the English but he couldn't answer back, just showed his hand in waiting signal.

Dicky nodded his head and kept waiting.

"Ou-Mi TO-Fu" a monk appeared about 5 minutes later and muttering Buddhist blessing.

"Are you monk Shih Lin?" said Dick Williams.

The monk in his early sixties nodded his head in a very silence manner.

"I had call you a short while before and I would like to make an appointment with you, my name is Dick Williams, a friend of Jean Clinton." Dick explained in English together with even childish gestures.

The monk didn't show any expressions, just raided his hand to invite Dicky to go into the temple.

Monk Shih Lin turned his body and heading to the inner hall of the temple.

Dick was ready to follow him, but the monk turned his head back to show Dicky to take off his shoes.

Dicky just realized that the monk was barefooted.

He obeyed the monk and left his shoes at the entrance side.

Shih Lin led him to the side room of the main hall where was the meeting room like place. He sat on the chairman's seat and pointed to the seat by his left side and invited Dicky to sit down.

Shih Lin knocked a copper made small bell on the table and about minutes later, a Spanish like middle aged nun appeared and sat just opposite to Dicky.

"Mr. Dick Williams, my name is Shih Ana, I'm the resident nun in the temple, I am from South Africa since Fu Kung temple has worldwide branched his sites, I'm here to help you." The blue eyes nun opened her mouth breaking the silence.

"How can I call you? Lady. I know nothing about Buddhist manners."

"Just call me Shih Ana, Shih is the surname for all the monks and nuns since we had abandoned our original surnames as soon as we accepted Buddhist religion.' Monk sat quietly just listening.

"Shih Ana, what I want to ask Shih Lin is that if he knows something about the Chinaman." Dicky took out directly the picture of the wanted guy.

Shih Ana passed the picture to Shih Lin and said something in Chinese to Shih Lin.

Monk Shih Lin studied the picture for a while then gave back it to Dicky.

He shook his head, then unioned his both palms and said, "OU MI TO FU"

"Shit! This fucking monk is smart!" Dicky said into his own belly.

"The master knows nothing about this man, sir." Shih Ana added.

The young man appeared again and served Dicky Argentine mineral water.

"Thank you." Dicky said, "By the way, for my personal curiosity, is the mineral water from supermarket?"

"Yes, Mr. Williams, we City temple people drink mineral water in stead of mountain spring water." Shih Ana explained to Dicky assisted with her sexy blue eyes.

Dicky noticed her even wide opened collar cut, the snow color plumped breasts almost floating out of her Buddhist suit.

"Really, it's quite interesting." Dicky avoided her looks.

Monk Shih Lin said something in Chinese to Shih Ana, then he got up and left the table while he showed again his OU MI TO FU blessing.

"Monk Shih Lin has an important appointment and he has to leave now, I would like to show you our temple. Mr.

Williams, if you would like to see?" Shih Ana said to Dicky with a charming smile.

"With pleasure, Shih Ana." Dicky got up from his seat, but the monk had left quickly.

"Shit." Dicky said again to himself.

"This way, please." Shih Ana got up ready to lead Dicky to visit the whole temple.

"We have five floors in this building, you want to see one by one?" Shih Ana showed the way to go to the entrance of the staircase, it was located behind one mirror like secret door.

Dicky followed Ana to raise along the wooden stairway, her ripe hips and huge ass was swimming together with her gray color Buddhist suit.

Dick even was attracted by her at the moment.

Ana showed Dicky floor by floor while they walked together into the inner parts of the building, it was real a fucking temple, every story contained different kinds of usage devices, meditation rooms, praying rooms, Yuga exercising rooms, bible reserving rooms, auditory, dinner room, monk's bed rooms, public bathing rooms, video cinema room, conference room, chief monk's office, officer's office, main salon, it was quite luxurious comparing Argentine current standard way of living, they met dozens personnel during the way.

They reached the top floor at last, it was a pure quiet floor with different closed rooms.

Sandalwood incense fragrance was floating in the air.

"I'd show you a very special place, do you want to see? Mr. Williams."

Ana said to Dicky with secret smile.

"With pleasure, lady.'

"Then just follow me!" Ana was heading to the end of wooden floor corridor.

Dicky went on and following her sexy ass, Ana reached the right door at the end, then pushed it in.

She stood by the entrance of the door and invited Dicky to go in.

Dicky stepped in and Ana followed meanwhile she closed and locked the door behind her.

Dicky found a wooden floor not small empty room except one thick and soft bed couch.

"Please sit down and relax yourself. Mr. Williams." Ana sat first on the couch.

Dicky obeyed since he got rather surprised.

"This is our VIP's massage room specially for our guests." Ana explained.

"Yes, it's very nice." Dicky sat on the soft couch and intended to make comfortable himself.

"Take off all your clothes just as I do!" Ana removed her suit right in a short second that made Dicky got no time to avoid it.

She was completely made herself naked.

The snow white flesh, plumped breasts, wide-forested big pussy, she stared at Dicky and widely apart her legs.

"Are you real Buddhist? lady."

"Of course, sir. We are of most modern and nature one."

"Come on, gentleman, take off your pants and let's have a good time.'

Ana neared Dicky and helped him to make himself quickly Adam.

"Why not? What a hot bitch!" Dicky accepted meanwhile saying to himself.

Dicky was hot enough he decided to screw this fucking false nun immediately.

"Don't hurry, gentleman. Let me make you first a Buddhist way massage, all right?"

"Just lay on your back and I'll make you feel better.'

Ana helped Dicky to lie loosely on the couch.

She got up and went to the side closet to bring massage oil, her harvest Latin shape made Dicky to rise suddenly his animal desire.

"You have to relax enough before you are going to eat me, right?" Ana began to work around Dick's neck, her fat breasts almost massaged Dick's neck smoothly meanwhile applying the oil she just took out from the wall side drawer.

Dick just felt a kind of heat invading straightly into her skin.

Ana went on rubbing her body, part by part down to his belly.

Her hands were soft and gentle.

Dicky could not wait one second more to make his penetration.

His thought just past, but his brain fell into the darkness all of a sudden.

The harvest sexy body of Ana fell into the infinite darkness as well.

Dicky found himself lain on the sidewalk near an old park under the afternoon sun, it was about 3 p.m., The park was almost empty excepting a few retired guys were playing chess on the stone made table and stools.

"Donde estamos, senor?" Dicky asked a workman like middle aged native fellow.

"Avenida de Las Incas, senor." The passenger answered him kindly and paid an attentive glance at Dicky since Dicky was sitting on the floor and his face was not quiet.

Dicky got up from the sidewalk, first he tried to orient his position, then he took the avenue heading to an old restaurant along the road.

"What a fucking dirty bitch, she betrayed me!" Dicky insulted her into his belly.

"And what a fucking day I've got!" he added.

Dick Williams found a telephone booth nearby and dialed Fu Kung Temple's number, but the Telephone Company just informed that, the number he had marked was the number out of it's service, then he intended to connect with Jean Clinton by phone, he private secretary just told him the CEO will not be in the office until next Wednesday as she had just left for Cordoba province by plane about 800 kilometers from B.A. City.

"Shit!" he paid the phone ticket then rushed out of the shop.

He took a cab, ordered the tachero to send him back to downtown.

"You Americano?" the corn mouth like driver intended to start the chatting.

"Yes," Dicky had no enough interest to talk with anybody.

"Vd. Saber your country is a "gran hijo de puta""

"You 'controlando' the FMI and 'hace' our country 'probe'."

The tachero said to Dicky in Spanish and English mixed language.

"Why don't you go to ask George W. Bush?"

Dick showed his impatience.

"George W. Bush is no good, you know?" the tachero turned his head back and stared at Dicky through his Mafioso like dark sunglasses seeming to wait Dick's answer.

"Look, why don't you take me directly to my destination and please don't "Hencha Belotas'."

Dick said even very unhappily.

"Si, senor . . ." the tachero understood the last word and switched on his radio in a rather loud voice then heading to Avenida de Mayo 654, 4 Piso at his maximum speed.

About 20 minutes later, he arrived to the place he wanted.

Dicky paid 20 pesos to the tachero, he received the money and said, "Muchisimos gracias, senor. Vd. Saber you Americanos took our money out and made a nosotros mas probe . . ."

"Shit!" Dicky closed the rear car door and left.

Dicky stepped on the entrance of the security counter who sent him to the 4h floor.

He pressed the elevator's button and the bird cage arrived at the 4th floor in a very short 4 seconds.

The entrance way of the 4th floor was in middle size like most of the commercial films have.

A full belly cop was reading the newspaper at desk, he looked at Dicky with questioning stares.

"I would like to see Mr. Director of the Office, sir." Dicky said to the policeman as soon as he neared the desk.

"De parte de quien?" the middle aged cop went on with his cross words with a fucking blue ball point pen.

"I don't know exactly, but Miss Jean Clinton send me here."

"Matha . . . !" the cop called aloud to the door inside.

A middle aged Chinese Argentine mixed woman appeared about 5 minutes stood by the electronic controlled semi transparent glass door. She was a slim woman near her fifties, her foxy smile made Dicky felt a little uneasy.

"Si, senor. Que desea?" she asked Dicky from a distance.

"Do you speak English? Lady."

"Yes, I do, Que busca?" Matha answered in her best Argentina English.

"Shit!" Dicky fucked himself into his own belly.

"I would like to see your Director General of the office."

"De parte de quien?" Matha didn't open the door yet.

"I don't know exactly, just tell your boss Jean Clinton sent me here."

"Who is Jean Clinton?"

"You don't know Jean Clinton? She is the cousin of President Bill Clinton." Dick got no way then, he threw her a lie.

"Oh, very good, please just wait for a few minutes, the Director is with some very important persons, would you 'pasar agui' and to have some café?"

Matha opened widely the door to invite Dicky in.

Matha led Dicky in and arranged him to sit on a sofa in the inner salon.

The reception waiting room was simple and clean, no any political air but rather officially heavy.

After near 30 minutes waiting, Matha appeared again asking Dicky to follow her to see the Director.

"Mr. Ambassador, here is Mr. Dick Williams, he is a distant cousin of Bill

Clinton." Matha presented him to a middle aged man who was standing in a distance welcoming Dicky with a political smile.

Dicky sat on a nice leather sofa after the Ambassador.

"So, Mr. Williams, you are the relative of bill Clinton." The man asked him in Chinese English.

"I've just said my friend Jean Clinton, maybe she is the distant cousin of Mr. Bill Clinton, anyway, I don't know Mr. Clinton personally." Matha came in and served Chinese green tea.

"That's all right, how can I help you anyway?"

"Oh, I'm here to see if your office could give me some information about this man."

Dicky passed the picture to the Director.

"Unfortunately I can't give you any information concerning this person, we have over 25,000 Chinese population who are living in this City.'

"Maybe you could give me some idea where I can get information?"

"I'm sorry, Mr. Williams, maybe Chinese Embassy could help you, I'm terrible sorry sir." The Director got up and ready to see Dicky off.

"Then, thank you for your time."

Dicky got no way, then he decided to leave the office.

Matha sat on her desk outside the director's office, she was calling and chatting with somebody and didn't notice Dicky's leaving.

It was near 4:30 p.m. when Dicky left the building and went to walk around Florida street, the most famous tourist path during her good time around 1970s.

Florida street today is a cheap sale market, 10 pesos here, 5 pesos there, some street side stands, even some street wonderers were trying their lucky.

"Senor, you have 50 cents, I need it for a bus ride.'

"Shit!" Dicky looked at a well dressed young man, he felt nasty and gave him no shit.

He stepped into a street side café, he needed a break.

"Sandwich and beer." he ordered the young waiter.

The shop was quiet and romantic like most of B.A.'s cafés.

Dicky sat down, his thoughts traveling around these few days fucking life.

"What shit is this?" he even didn't understand for himself.

The young waiter neared him again and brought his order.

"Puedo sentarme senor?" a whore like tall girl in her early thirties looked at him with seductive glances.

"Yes, you may." Dicky was really tired, he instantly raised a bit of sex desire.

The girl sat on the chair opposite him as soon as she got the permission.

"You want something for drinking?" Dick stared her low cut huge breasts.

"Yes, I need a big cheese and ham sandwich and 100 pesos, then let's go to the hotel crossing the street, you pay the room and you can do what you want with me." The girl was hungry and straight.

"Mozo, bring me a sandwich of 'jamon y queso' and a beer like this."

Dick Williams had a very bad day he wanted to make a quick relax.

The young waiter served what he ordered and left.

The girl ate the sandwich like a real hungry cat.

"Are you Americano?" she bite with full mouth and accompanied with the beer.

"Yes, and then, what? Finish your food and drink, then let's go to bed."

"No, for Americano, 200 pesos." The girl raised the price according to the river level.

"You want 200 pesos, I'll give you 200 pesos." Dick began to feel pity for her poorness.

He took the girl across the street and went into a three stories hotel.

"Buenas trades, senor, you want a room?" the counter clerk said to him with a secret smile.

"Yes, give me a double room with bathroom.'

"You want for through the night or only for 2 hours resting?"

"Give a room for tonight." He changed the idea.

"Is the lady your wife, sir?" the clerk intended to catch the tip.

"How much is the rate?"

"We charge 50 dollars for a double room."

"Take 60 dollars and give me the key.'

"Sure, sir.'

"My name is Roberto, when you check out tomorrow morning, just ask for me." Roberto took off the room key from the stand and passed it to Dicky.

"How, you don't give receipt?"

"No, senor, we can't give you a receipt if la senorita will go in with you."

Roberto said to Dicky meanwhile he glanced the hooker.

"Room 202, take the staircase to the second floor, it's on your left hand.'

"You got no elevator?"

"We don't use elevator since 1950."

"Shit!" Dicky took the hooker's hand heading to the upstairs room.

"The hotel room was big enough, quiet and decorated in European classic fashion.

The hooker began to undress herself as soon as they stepped into the room.

"Wait, just sit down, I want to talk with you first.'

"How, you don't want to fuck me now?"

The girl was anxious to finish the business.

"Sit down, tell me what's your name?' Dicky sat on his back on one side of the couch.

"What's your care if my name is Morica or Margarita?"

The girl threw herself on the couch too.

"You don't really look like a professional hooker, maybe you just need money urgently, that doesn't matter, what I need is to through tonight with somebody.' Dicky looked deeply inside the girl's eyes.

"You have a pair of beautiful eyes." He added.

"My name is Vicky, you don't look like a fucker neither, you look like a gent."

Vicky threw her half part of long hair over her right shoulder.

"You want to stay with me for the whole night, I could pay you for the time." Dicky pulled her lift hand and made her lie on his left breast.

"If you want me for the whole night, then I should charge you for the full night." Vicky said to Dick.

"How much will it cost?'

"Two hundred U.S. dollars.'

"You got it!" Dick said in no hesitate.

"Then give me two hundred dollars right now, you can begin to enjoy me up to tomorrow morning afterwards." Vicky said with a little bitterness and business like.

Dick jumped out of the bed and took out two green notes to give them to Vicky.

The hooker received them first kept them into her purse, then began to undress her hot pants.

"Don't do it now, first you go to bath and we could play later on.

"You're a strange guy, you see." Vicky got up and obeyed Dicky's order.

She went into the bath room.

Dicky switched on the music system, then raised the tube and ordered champagne room service.

Vicky came out from the john in her full nudity her ripe shape made Dicky felt really passionate.

"Put something on and sign for me if the room service come.

Dicky got up heading to the bathroom.

He opened the cold shower intending to wash whole his dirtiness and depression after these few days fucking life.

He took a long shower, it took him more than 20 minutes.

Dicky dried himself, then put the white hotel robe, he lazily came out of the bathroom.

The hotel room was silent as a cemetery, nobody was in, included the girl named herself Vicky about half an hour ago.

The door was knocked.

"Who is it?"

"Room service, senor.' A low male voice came from outside the room door,

He opened the door, a dark waiter in his early thirties pushed the cart in with a smart and service smile.

"Did you see my girl in this room?"

"Which girl? Senor, I didn't see any girl."

"How? She was just in here." Dicky felt even desperate.

"Did you lose anything? Senor.' The waiter began to serve the champagne and saying with attention.

"Oh, shit, my wallet, my credit cards." Dicky just found that his personal belongings had swept away without saying goodbye.

"Shit, fucking whore!" Dicky was even furious.

"Never trust a whore, senor." the waiter felt uncomfortable and intended to console Dicky.

Dicky signed the ticket and said, "Put 10% for your tip. I'll call my friend to come to clean the account."

"Thank you, senor. By the way, you want a 'chica', I can bring you a girl, young, clean and in good shape, you could pay her in pesos, it's cheap, only $30."

"Well, send me any girl who got a vagina, I need a quick fuck, I am going to blow out, you see.'

Dick took out his last 100 pesos from his leather belt, he handed it to the waiter.

"The girl will be here in five minutes, senor." The waiter took the money then left behind the room door.

A dark and fat girl in her early twenties came into the room, she said 'Hola' to Dicky, then took off her pants and red slip together.

Dick threw her straightly on to the bed, then hungrily rode on her, he made a dozen times powerful strokes then collapse on her half nuked body.

Dicky got up from her body then gestured her to leave the room.

He went to the bathroom, washed himself well, he felt instantly relaxed.

He lay on the bed, then fell into sleep.

When Dicky woke up it was the next morning, he took the table phone, called the Dutchman.

"What happened? Mr. Williams, it still so early."

The wall clock pointed 7 a.m.

"Any news?" Dutchman added.

"No, sir, what I need is some money, I lost all my things in my hotel room, I can't check out without a penny." Dicky said desperate.

"What's the check out time?"

"10 a.m."

"Tell me where you are and your phone number, I'll send my man to arrange it, you just leave the place, that's all." Dutchman cut the phone.

"Shit! What a shame!" Dicky got up and prepare to leave the hotel.

Telephone rang.

He took the phone off, "Yes.?"

"Dicky, is that you? It's me, Diana. I'm calling you from Mexico City, are you all right?"

"I'm living in a terrible mess, what hell is that? You got my hotel room number?"

"I've told you, I'm caring after you, look, if you need money, you could go to Banco De Boston, central house, just ask Miss Linda Hess, she's the chief of the banking system, ask her how much cash you want, of course, no excess 5,000 dollars.'

"What shit is this? Diana." Dicky really fell into a puzzle poor.

"I see you, Dicky."

"Shit!"

It was a sunny morning, Dicky went out from the hotel walking along the Diogonal Norte avenue, he was looking for Banco de Boston, he found the place after asking several passengers, Argentine people were kind on answering questions specially for the foreign or people who really don't know well the streets or place names.

Linda Hess was an American woman in her early thirties, tall, elegant and professionally kind in speaking and attention.

Dicky Williams met Linda in her head office located at a middle size room on the second floor.

She listened, then opened the drawer by her left knee, took out a check book, she wrote something on the paper, and closed the book back, she passed the paper slip to Dicky saying, "Please go to the basement cash window No.5, the cashier will pay you the amount of cash.'

"It's 5,000 U.S. dollars, lady.' Dicky read the ticket.

"Yes, we will discount it from your federal account in B.A., that's all."

Linda Hess rose up and ready to see Dicky off.

"Thanks a lot, lady.'

"You're welcome.'

Linda went back to sit and raised the phone tube for continuing her work.

Dicky Williams arrived to his apartment near Plaza Italia, it was already 10 p.m. since everything he intended to find out were in vain.

He passed the long and dark corridor, took the bird cage, then reached the flat door.

He put the key, unlocked it in his usually way, what he found was a great surprise.

The whole flat was completely empty.

It was pure naked.

"What this whole fuck? My God!" Dicky even couldn't find back his own phone.

He walked around the living, bedroom, kitchen and bathroom, there was nothing except quietness and lightings.

He found out at last an envelope putting on the kitchen sink side.

He opened it and read it over.

It was a simple 4A size white paper.

It written:

> *Dear Mr. Dick Williams,*
>   *Your mission is over and you are formally*
> *out of the Agency.*
>   *The file No.705 is officially cancelled.*
>   *Good luck!*

> *Dutchman*

"Son of bitch! What's all of this mess?"

Dicky was really running mad.

He found a small hotel nearby and passed through the night.

The night was long and very thoughtful.

He got up the next morning about 10 a.m., he ran to the nearest telephone booth along Santa Fe Avenue.

He called Diana Martinez, Jean Clinton, Charles Liu even Linda Hess.

The answers were all the same"

We never had this person in this office.

Dicky was really fed up.

What he still hold on hand was 5,000 U.S. dollars.

After a long hanging up at the sidewalk café, he got up and waved to a cab.

He got in the cab and ordered the driver to send him to Plaza Constitucion.

During the way, he was thinking, "Is Jackson Smith still living in St. Diego Church?"

Jackson Smith was his colleague during 1970s, they were sent together in B.A. to join Agency's operations in Argentina.

One year later, Dicky went back to Washington, Jackson Smith remained in B.A. for his task.

Two years later he received a letter from Jackson in B.A. saying that, he was going to resign and to settle down in the City, because everything in the world is a shit.

Two more years later, he received again a postcard from Jackson, he was living happily in B.A. and whenever Dick want to visit him in B.A. he could find him in St. Diego Church.

"You know Constitution Park? Ask anyone where is the church." Jacjson wrote in his last letter.

"Aca estamos, senor." The driver advised Dicky.

Dicky was almost failing deeply in his thoughts during the 20 minutes ride.

"Oh, it's O.K., cuando es?"

Dicky paid the driver, then got off from the cab.

Father Jackson Smith looked elder than his age when Dicky met him at St. Diego Church after almost 25 years separation.

They even could not recognize reach other before they exchanged their names. 25 years is a long time that could rose one new born baby up to a well educated Ph.D.

Jackson invited Dicky to the restaurant nearby to celebrate their reunion, during the three hours food and wine, Jackson asked what was really the reason that brought him to visit him.

Dicky told everything that had happened during the past few days and still get no answer, why he was suddenly out of the Agency?

"Look, Dick. I'm a long time being the outsider of the Company, I've got my peaceful life in B.A. after I had resigned from the Company 20 years ago. I am a true father now although I don't really believe in god, but this Church gave me a good fucking life, I have my economic basis, my healthy sexual life with women, and most certainly, I'm really outside the miserable agent-life.

It's the right time for you to jump out of the fucking field, of course, you don't quite understand what was the real reason why you are betrayed by the Company? But sometimes, it's better to look back to the past." Jackson talked really like a religious Father.

"But who was the person who did me so?"

"It's not important anymore."

"Is my chief Tompson who did it?"

"No, he is just a piece of the chess."

"Is Dutchman's guilty?"

"No, he's also a piece of a chess."

"How about the ladies I had mentioned to you? Diana Martinez, Christian Anderson, Jean Clinton, Linda

Hess? Who's the Chinaman they wanted me to find out? Who is Charles Lee, another Chinaman?"

"They are all on the same boat."

"I have been a long time in the Company, Jackson. I behaved always well."

"But they want you to go off the board now." Jackson took out his pipe from the pants side pocket began to lit it up.

"Dick, please don't go on to dig the mess, it's the time to leave the Company, just leave everything and get out of the trouble, you understand me?'

"What can I do now? Go back to Virginia my home town?"

"Go back there if you still want, otherwise you could bring your wife and sons here, I got a piece of land and a country house 300 miles to the south, you could stay there for a period of time.' Jackson patted Dick's hand on the café table.

"You know who is the man behind all of this? Jackson."

"He is the Boss, you know. Nobody can go against him except you put your own life."

"The Boss, Jackson." Dick smiled and relaxed.

"That's why you gave yourself up twenty years ago and live in this fucking place up to now.'

"No, Dick, this is not a fucking place, this is a beautiful land, the problem of this country is because they have too many bosses."

"I just made up my mind to go back to Virginia right tomorrow and maybe I'll come with my family a few months later."

"That's my boy." Jackson smiled pleasantly.

"Come on, come to my church, I'll show you what I got in my place."

– THE END –